leapfrog
Rhyme
Time

Felicity Floss: Tooth Fairy

by Maeve Friel

Illustrated by Sarah Horne

W
FRANKLIN WATTS
LONDON•SYDNEY

My name's Felicity Floss.
Hello!

I've been the tooth fairy
since ages ago.

My job is keeping
all of you happy,

6

while your smiles
are looking gappy.

But now I hear some
of you lisping:

"I've been wobbed!
My toof's gone missing!"

I must agree
it's not very funny,

to lose a tooth
and get no money.

11

But don't blame me,
whatever you do!

I'm just as cross
as any of you!

13

So, last night, while
you children slept,

I silently from my
toadstool crept ...

16

... to see for once
who was the thief,
stealing all your
pearly teeth.

17

I'd hardly left my fairy den to start my moonlit hunting, when ...

19

... down an alley

I heard a squeak

20

and saw a ratty

figure sneak ...

... nipping along on tippy toes, shiny white pearls all over his clothes.

23

Shiny white pearls?
Could they be teeth?

24

"Oi! DJ Pearly! You're the milk teeth thief!"

"C...c...cool it, Fliss!"
the rat spat back.

"Gleaming like this

is in my act!"

I whooshed my wand.
I said, "Take that!

To pay him back for
the teeth he took,
what did I do?
Well, just look!

Leapfrog has been specially designed to fit the requirements of the National Literacy Strategy. It offers real books for beginning readers by top authors and illustrators.

There are 43 Leapfrog stories to choose from:

The Bossy Cockerel
ISBN 0 7496 3828 1

Bill's Baggy Trousers
ISBN 0 7496 3829 X

Mr Spotty's Potty
ISBN 0 7496 3831 1

Little Joe's Big Race
ISBN 0 7496 3832 X

The Little Star
ISBN 0 7496 3833 8

The Cheeky Monkey
ISBN 0 7496 3830 3

Selfish Sophie
ISBN 0 7496 4385 4

Recycled!
ISBN 0 7496 4388 9

Felix on the Move
ISBN 0 7496 4387 0

Pippa and Poppa
ISBN 0 7496 4386 2

Jack's Party
ISBN 0 7496 4389 7

The Best Snowman
ISBN 0 7496 4390 0

Eight Enormous Elephants
ISBN 0 7496 4634 9

Mary and the Fairy
ISBN 0 7496 4633 0

The Crying Princess
ISBN 0 7496 4632 2

Jasper and Jess
ISBN 0 7496 4081 2

The Lazy Scarecrow
ISBN 0 7496 4082 0

The Naughty Puppy
ISBN 0 7496 4383 8

Freddie's Fears
ISBN 0 7496 4382 X

Cinderella
ISBN 0 7496 4228 9

The Three Little Pigs
ISBN 0 7496 4227 0

Jack and the Beanstalk
ISBN 0 7496 4229 7

The Three Billy Goats Gruff
ISBN 0 7496 4226 2

Goldilocks and the Three Bears
ISBN 0 7496 4225 4

Little Red Riding Hood
ISBN 0 7496 4224 6

Rapunzel
ISBN 0 7496 6159 3

Snow White
ISBN 0 7496 6161 5

The Emperor's New Clothes
ISBN 0 7496 6163 1

The Pied Piper of Hamelin
ISBN 0 7496 6164 X

Hansel and Gretel
ISBN 0 7496 6162 3

The Sleeping Beauty
ISBN 0 7496 6160 7

Rumpelstiltskin
ISBN 0 7496 6153 4*
ISBN 0 7496 6165 8

The Ugly Duckling
ISBN 0 7496 6154 2*
ISBN 0 7496 6166 6

Puss in Boots
ISBN 0 7496 6155 0*
ISBN 0 7496 6167 4

The Frog Prince
ISBN 0 7496 6156 9*
ISBN 0 7496 6168 2

The Princess and the Pea
ISBN 0 7496 6157 7*
ISBN 0 7496 6169 0

Dick Whittington
ISBN 0 7496 6158 5*
ISBN 0 7496 6170 4

Squeaky Clean
ISBN 0 7496 6588 2*
ISBN 0 7496 6805 9

Craig's Crocodile
ISBN 0 7496 6589 0*
ISBN 0 7496 6806 7

Felicity Floss: Tooth Fairy
ISBN 0 7496 6590 4*
ISBN 0 7496 6807 5

Captain Cool
ISBN 0 7496 6591 2*
ISBN 0 7496 6808 3

Monster Cake
ISBN 0 7496 6592 0*
ISBN 0 7496 6809 1

The Super Trolley Ride
ISBN 0 7496 6593 9*
ISBN 0 7496 6810 5

* hardback